ALLISON'S GRANDFATHER

ALLISON'S GRANDFATHER

by Linda Peavy
Illustrations by Ronald Himler

Published by Charles Scribner's Sons / New York

Library of Congress Cataloging in Publication Data
Peavy, Linda   Allison's grandfather.
Summary: A young child thinks about her friend's
grandfather's death.
[1. Death—Fiction] I. Himler, Ronald. II. Title
PZ7.P33Al   [E]   81-2297
ISBN 0-684-17017-5   AACR 2

1 3 5 7 9 11 13 15 17 19 Q D/C 20 18 16 14 12 10 8 6 4 2

Printed in the United States of America

To the tough magic of
Jane Forsythe and Jane Yolen

Allison's grandfather was dying. Erica knew because Allison's grandmother had told Mama. But did Allison know? Erica had wondered about that all morning. She knew how much Allison loved her grandfather, and she worried that since Allison lived so far away she might not know he was ill. Erica wanted to ask Mama whether Allison knew, but she really didn't feel like talking about dying. Not just yet.

In fact, she did not even like to think about Allison's grandfather dying. How was he doing it? Was it very, very hard to die? Or was it easy? Mama said he was in the hospital, so he wasn't dying up on the ranch.

Erica remembered Allison's grandfather on the ranch. He hadn't been dying then. Last June when Allison had flown from somewhere far away to spend the summer with her grandparents, she had been lonely. Her grandfather had decided she needed a friend and had invited Erica to come up to the ranch and spend several weekends with them.

The ranch was beautiful, with the mountains stretching up, up, up behind the house, behind the cabins, and behind the corral where horses used to be. The horses had been sold long ago, but the blankets in the barn still smelled like horses. The girls had ridden on a saddle Allison's grandfather had tied to an old barrel. Then, in late afternoons, the three of them had sat on the top rail of the corral and watched the clouds turn different shades of pink as the sun dipped over the mountains. Still later in the evenings, the two friends had sat by the fire and listened to the stories Allison's grandfather told about his days as a cowboy.

"I was no dime store cowboy," he almost always said at the start of a story. "No, sir, I was the real thing." Erica didn't know exactly what Allison's grandfather meant

when he said that, but she liked to look at the faded brown-tone pictures of rodeos and roundups he showed them. And she liked to listen to the stories, even though she didn't always understand all the words.

Allison, who had heard all her grandfather's stories already, didn't seem to worry about the words she didn't understand. She was so used to the way he always started his stories that she would tell Erica to sit still and get ready to listen whenever she saw him take down his silver spurs from their hook over the fireplace. Sure enough, more than once he had brought the spurs over to the girls, handed one to Erica, and said, "Bet you never saw anything like this before. Hand-crafted silver spurs. Real silver. Just look at the way they shine."

After that, he would sit down and start another story. Soon Erica grew used to sitting and watching Allison's grandfather spin the wheel of one silver spur with his finger as he told about being a real cowboy. "Yes, sir, little girls," he would say with a far-away smile on his face, "this old cowboy liked nothing better than to saddle up Nugget and ride up into those mountains to look for strays."

It was easy to watch the wheel of the silver spur spinning as Allison's grandfather talked about riding over the mountains. And it was easy to listen to what he said, since his stories were full of adventure. Like the time he had been surprised by a mother bear and two cubs while gathering gooseberries on Wapiti Creek early one August morning.

"I ran one way and that big she-bear ran another," Allison's grandfather laughed. "By the time I stopped to catch my breath, I'd lost all but a handful of that bucketful of berries. Still, I guess no pancakes ever tasted any better than the ones I made with Mama Bear's gooseberries."

"I like blueberry pancakes," Erica said, "but I've never

even *heard* of gooseberry pancakes."

"Never heard of gooseberry pancakes?" Allison's grandfather said with surprise. "Well, we'll just have to have some for supper the next time you come up," he promised.

Erica didn't really believe they would, since grownups are always making promises they forget about. But Allison's grandfather didn't forget. As Erica followed Allison into the kitchen the very next Friday evening, she heard the sizzle of batter being poured onto a hot griddle.

"I was up the creek at daybreak after these berries," said Allison's grandfather as he sprinkled a handful of fat gooseberries onto the bubbling batter. "Found plenty of 'em, too," he continued, motioning toward the large bucket on the countertop by the stove. "But I was awful disappointed that Mama Bear didn't come out to help me pick this time."

Although they had only had gooseberry pancakes once last summer, Allison's grandfather had told them the story of the bear and the berries many, many times. Grandfathers do that. They seem to enjoy telling the same stories over and over. Erica wondered about that, but she didn't ever ask about it. Instead, she just listened a little less carefully to the stories she knew the best.

Most of Allison's grandfather's stories were exciting, even when they'd been told again and again. Especially the one about nearly freezing to death one winter. He'd been up at the ranch alone and decided he would have to lead the horses down through the snow to the valley because all their hay was gone. The day was so cold his breath froze in the air and his feet were numb in his boots, but the horses had to be moved. He'd tied them together, one horse's halter to the next horse's tail, so that he could ride Nugget, hold the bridle of the next horse, and move the

whole string, nose to tail, down the mountain.

"Just as we were moving onto the main road," Allison's grandfather said, "Nugget slipped and fell, throwing me out of the saddle so I was caught halfway under her. Worse yet, my left foot had gone clean through the stirrup and was wedged deep in the snow.

"I was scared, little girls, mighty scared," he said as he spun the wheel of his silver spur, "but I just talked gentle to that horse and held that bridle hard against her nose so she wouldn't move. I knew she'd want to be on her feet again real soon and then I'd be in trouble. I'd be dragged in the snow until I froze to death or got run in by that string of cold and hungry horses. I had to get the saddle loose so I could pull my leg free.

"I worked at that cinch real gentle and quiet, easing it out until I felt the saddle start to slip. Suddenly, I felt Nugget's muscles tighten. She was going to get on her feet again. Time was running out—fast. Then, at the very moment that horse struggled up, the saddle fell free. I just lay there for a while, a man mighty happy to be alive.

"Yes, sir, little girls, Old Man Death got surprised that day. Thought he had me for sure, figured I'd be froze stiff. But I wasn't ready to die that day, little girls, I wasn't ready to die."

Erica wondered whether Allison's grandfather was ready to die now. He hadn't said so last summer, but he hadn't been sick last summer. Now Mama said he was very, very sick.

When you were so sick you couldn't get well, were you ready to die? How could you be sure when you got that sick? Did Allison's grandfather still remember that day in the mountains when he hadn't been ready to die?

Erica wanted to ask Mama just when Allison's grandfather had decided he was ready to die, but she really didn't feel like asking about dying. Not just yet. She knew grandfathers died. One of her own grandfathers had died before she was born, and she only knew about him from his pictures. In one picture he was playing a fiddle, and she wondered what the music sounded like.

But Papa, Erica's other grandfather, was safe and well way down South. Papa had promised to come for her birthday next summer. He called her on the telephone and sent funny letters with pictures in them. She sent pictures to him and signed her name herself.

Erica thought about Allison's being so far away while her grandfather was dying. She wondered whether anyone would tell her if Papa got sick. She thought someone probably would, but she didn't really want to ask about that. Not just now.

Instead, she helped Mama fill the bird feeder and shovel snow from the sidewalk. Then she drew pictures to

send to Papa. Mama wrote a letter to go with the pictures, and they put everything in an envelope with a stamp on it. Then, just before supper, she and Daddy walked to the corner together to mail the letter. She wanted to ask whether Mama had put anything in the letter about Allison's grandfather, but instead she asked Daddy to help her build a snow baby.

When it was time for bed that night, Erica was surprised to see Mama put on her heavy coat and snow boots. "Where are you going?" she asked.

"I'm going to the hospital to sit with Allison's grandfather tonight," Mama explained as she gave her a hug and a kiss.

"Why are you going to sit with him, Mama?" Erica asked. "Won't he be asleep since it's nighttime? Especially since he's sick?"

"Yes, he will be sleeping," Mama answered, "but he

likes having someone hold his hand while he sleeps, and Allison's grandmother has been there all day. She wants to go home and call Allison's mother, and she needs to get plenty of rest tonight."

After Mama had gone, Erica lay and thought about why Allison's grandfather wanted someone to hold his hand. Last summer he hadn't wanted someone to do that. But last summer he hadn't been dying. Last summer he had been carrying buckets of gooseberries in his big, strong hands. Or using his hands to help them into the saddle. Or to spin the wheel of his silver spur. Or to wipe away Allison's tears the day she stuck a fish hook in her finger.

That night Allison's grandfather's hands were busy in Erica's dreams. She did not dream of his hands being still and asleep. She had not ever seen them being still.

When Erica woke up, the sun was shining through the frost on the window. A chickadee was cracking sunflower

seeds in the feeder on the sill. Erica felt fresh and happy. For a moment she almost forgot about Allison's grandfather. She sat up in bed, put her feet in her slippers, and started into the bedroom to give Mama a hug. But Mama wasn't there. Then Erica remembered. She wanted to ask Daddy about Allison's grandfather, but instead she said, "When is Mama coming home?"

"Very soon," Daddy answered. "I just called her. Let's go down and make a surprise breakfast for her."

Down in the kitchen Erica and Daddy fixed eggs and pancakes. Erica watched Daddy's hands turning the pancakes. She thought of gooseberry pancakes and of Allison's grandfather's hands and of Mama holding his hand while he was dying in the night. But she didn't say anything about that to Daddy. Instead, she asked again, "When's Mama coming?" and helped set the knives and forks and napkins on the table.

Just as Daddy was pouring the orange juice, Erica heard the front door open. She ran to the door and hugged Mama tightly. She held on for a long time. She did not want to let go.

"And how is my little girl?" Mama asked with a smile. "Did you sleep well?"

"Yes, but you didn't sleep, did you?" Erica asked.

"No, I didn't sleep," Mama answered as she took off her coat, "but I can sleep later today."

Daddy came from the kitchen and gave Mama a long, long hug without saying anything. Erica wanted to ask whether Allison's grandfather had finished dying yet, but instead she said, "Come see the breakfast surprise, Mama."

When breakfast was over, Mama put the dishes in the sink, then sat in the big green chair near the window seat. She leaned her head back, closed her eyes, and began to rock. She looked very, very tired. Erica wanted to ask if it had been hard to stay awake all night, but instead she climbed into Mama's lap and snuggled very close to her. They rocked and rocked without saying anything, and Erica felt warm and good.

Finally, Mama stopped rocking and answered the question Erica hadn't yet asked. "Allison's grandfather died this morning at six o'clock."

Erica didn't look up but snuggled still closer. They rocked and rocked without words for a while. Erica tried to think of Allison's grandfather dead, but she had never even seen him sick and so she could not think how he would be dead. She rocked and rocked and thought and thought. Then she asked, "Were you holding his hand when he died, Mama?"

"Yes," said Mama as she rocked.

"How did it feel to be holding his hand when he died?" Erica asked.

"It was all right, Erica," Mama said softly. "It was even beautiful. He opened his eyes and looked straight at me and smiled. Then he died."

"How was it to die?" Erica asked.

"He just stopped breathing. The nurse came in and listened with a stethoscope and said that his heart had stopped beating," Mama explained.

They rocked and rocked for a long, long time without words again.

Finally, Erica asked, "But why did he smile, Mama?"

"I don't really know," Mama answered, "but I like to think it was because he was somehow riding over the mountains again instead of lying in that hospital knowing he couldn't be well. The part of him that's light and life was suddenly riding over the mountains once again."

Erica thought about that. Allison's grandfather couldn't really be riding his horse. Not if he were dead.

But she liked to think of him riding and not just lying there being dead. She thought Allison would like that, too. She wondered what Allison had said when she was told about her grandfather. But she really didn't want to ask anything more about dying. Not out loud. Not just now.

Just now she wanted to rock and rock and think about Allison's grandfather riding across the mountains on the saddle that hung in the barn by the blankets that smelled like the horses that didn't live there anymore. Just now she wanted to think about Allison's grandfather riding over the mountains with the sunlight dancing and sparkling off his bright silver spurs.